★ BY DAVID ORME

ILLUSTRATED BY PAUL SAVAGE

Librarian Reviewer
Joanne Bongaarts
Educational Consultant
MS in Library Media Education, Minnesota State University, Mankato
Teacher and Media Specialist with Edina Public Schools, MN, 1993–2000

Reading Consultant
Elizabeth Stedem
Educator/Consultant, Colorado Springs, CO
MA in Elementary Education, University of Denver, CO

STONE ARCH BOOKS
Minneapolis   San Diego

First published in the United States in 2007
by Stone Arch Books, A Capstone Imprint
151 Good Counsel Drive, P.O. Box 669,
Mankato, Minnesota 56002.
www.capstonepub.com

Originally published in Great Britain in 2002
by Badger Publishing Ltd.

Library of Congress Cataloging-in-Publication Data
Orme, David, 1948 Mar. 1–

[Starship football]

Space Games / by David Orme; illustrated by Paul Savage.

p. cm. — (Keystone Books)

Originally published in Great Britain in 2002 under title: Starship
Football.

Summary: On board *The Searcher*, travelling through space, Todd
enlists the help of the ship's captain to create a soccer field in one
of the unused cargo holds so he and the other soccer fans can have
interplanetary matches.

ISBN-13: 978-1-59889-096-9 (hardcover)

ISBN-10: 1-59889-096-4 (hardcover)

ISBN-13: 978-1-59889-246-8 (paperback)

ISBN-10: 1-59889-246-0 (paperback)

[1. Soccer—Fiction. 2. Space flight—Fiction. 3. Science fiction.]
I. Savage, Paul, 1971– ill. II. Title. III. Series: Keystone books (Stone
Arch)
PZ7.O6338Sp 2007
[Fic]—dc22   2006004061

Printed in the United States of America in Stevens Point, Wisconsin.
042010
005756R

TABLE OF CONTENTS

CHAPTER 1

TODD'S PROBLEM

Todd knew that he was lucky. Most boys his age never went into space.

Todd's mom and dad were part of the crew on a huge starship. The ship, called *The Searcher,* went on missions across the galaxy.

There were nearly two thousand people on the ship. The crew could take their families with them.

There was always plenty to do on
the ship, but Todd and his friends had
a problem. They lived for the one thing
they couldn't do on the starship.

They loved soccer.

Of course, they could watch as much soccer as they wanted. All the big matches between planets were shown on the starship TV.

They could even play lots of virtual soccer.

To play virtual soccer, you put on a helmet and a special suit, and stood on a platform. As you moved around, the floor moved under you. You felt as if you were running around and kicking, just like in a real game. You didn't really move very far at all.

Todd's friends wanted to play real soccer, but there wasn't anywhere to play.

"You can't play real soccer on a starship," Todd's dad explained. "There's no room for a field."

CHAPTER 2

THE
ALL-STARS

Todd and his soccer-crazy friends made up a five player team they called "Searcher's All-Stars."

- Todd was forward.

- Mick and Tony played mid-field.

- Tim was big and beefy, so he was on defense.

- Becky was goalie.

One day, after school, they were sitting in the locker room. Captain Robins came in. Todd's friends were surprised.

The captain didn't often come into the locker room. He was much too important.

Becky knew the captain well. Her mother worked with him on the ship's bridge. The captain waved to her.

"Hello, kids," he said. "Finished with school for the day?"

Todd thought quickly. Maybe they could get the captain on their side.

"Excuse me, Captain Robins," he said. "We're the Searcher's All-Stars. We're crazy about soccer, but there's nowhere to play. Can you help?"

Captain Robins smiled. "I'm a soccer fan myself! I support the Galactic Waves! There's not much room on a starship, you know."

Todd groaned to himself. That was what his dad had said.

The captain went on. "Even if there was room, one team's no good. You need someone to play!"

CHAPTER 3

THE CHALLENGE

The captain was right. You need two teams for a soccer match.

The captain made a note of Todd's name. He said he would see what he could do, but what could he do when there was only one team and no room?

Todd was amazed when a message came from the captain three days later. He showed it to his parents.

CHALLENGE!

THE SEARCHER'S ALL STARS ARE CHALLENGED TO A SPECIAL

FIVE-A-SIDE

IN HOLD 5-C

ON THE FIRST SATURDAY THIS MONTH

CAPTAIN ROBINS
MANAGER, SEARCHER'S UNITED

Dad laughed. "Good old Captain Robins! Hold 5-C is empty on this trip. It's a big space, just right for soccer! Who are Searcher's United?" Dad asked.

Todd didn't know, but Becky did. She heard about it from her mom.

"The captain's really great. Some of the crew have played soccer before. They've made up a team to play us!" said Becky.

Playing against the crew? Todd wasn't sure about that. Some of the spacemen on the ship were very tough.

"What do we do?" asked Todd.

"Accept the challenge," said Tim. "We can't back out now."

Todd wrote to the captain and accepted the challenge. The captain wrote back, telling him that they could use Hold 5-C for team practice. He said that he would referee the game. He also promised to be fair.

CHAPTER 4

PRACTICE

The crew worked hard to turn the big, empty hold into a soccer field. Lines were painted on the floor, and goals had been set up. Right after school, the All-Stars had their first practice.

There were a few problems.

Todd knew all about soccer and the five-a-side rules. It wasn't the same as really playing.

Todd got the team to practice skills such as dribbling, passing the ball, and tackling, but they needed real game practice.

Everyone agreed that Becky was their best player. She didn't need to learn how to goal keep. She was a natural player.

Time and time again Todd fired the ball at the goal, but not much got past her. The All-Stars might not score many goals, but with Becky as the goalie, maybe the crew wouldn't either.

The final practice session had just finished. The match was tomorrow.

"One good thing," said Tony. "The hold is only big enough for the players. No one else will see how badly we do."

As they were leaving the hold, they met two crew members coming in. "What's going on?" asked Mick.

"We're setting up cameras," said one. "Everyone's so interested in the game that it's going to show live on ship TV. The whole ship will be watching."

The captain organized the game really well. Special soccer jerseys had been made. The All-Stars wore blue, with white stars. The United were in red, with a picture of *The Searcher* across their chests.

The crew team looked very big. Todd felt his knees shaking. He hoped it didn't show on TV!

Captain Robins wore referee's clothes. He asked Todd to shake hands with the captain of the crew's team.

The crew's captain was Charlie Burnet, who worked with Todd's dad. Charlie was really friendly. Todd felt better right away.

Todd kicked off, passing the ball to Tony. The plan was that Todd would run forward and Tony would pass it back to him. He would then shoot a quick goal before the other team could get themselves organized.

It didn't work out that way. Tony got the ball and passed it back, but Charlie Burnet intercepted the pass. Meanwhile, another United player was moving up.

Charlie crossed the ball to him.
Tony tried to tackle, but the player
sidestepped and shot at the goal.

Luckily, Becky was ready. She made
a great save, kicking the ball back up
the field to Mick. Mick tried to pass to
Todd. He tripped and lost the ball to a
United player.

The ball was soon back with
Charlie. This time he didn't pass.
Bang! He shot for a goal. Becky dived
desperately, but the ball was in the net.

By halftime it was clear that the All-Stars were going to lose.

United had already scored six goals. The All-Stars never even had a good shot at the goal.

At last they got a chance. It was all down to Becky. She kicked the ball really well, right to Todd's feet. The United goalie wasn't ready. Todd hammered the ball home.

CHAPTER 6

YOU'RE THE PROBLEM

When Captain Robins blew the final whistle the score was 9 - 1. The crew won.

Todd and his team put on a brave face. They thanked the captain and the crew, and said how much they enjoyed it. If only the game hadn't been shown over the whole ship.

Charlie Burnet was talking to the captain. He called Todd back.

"I'm really impressed with how well you organized your team," said Charlie. "You didn't give up even though you were losing."

"Thanks," said Todd, "but we weren't very good, were we?"

Captain Robins laughed. "You can't expect to be, yet. You know all about soccer, but you've never actually played before."

"You did very well for a first game, especially your goalie," added the captain. "I think Mr. Burnet has something else to say."

"That's right," said Charlie. "Now, do you know the main problem with your team?"

Todd shook his head.

"It's you! You try to do too much. You're trying to be the captain and the coach. Now, how about taking on a new coach?" said Charlie.

"Who?" asked Todd.

"Me!" said Charlie.

CHAPTER 7

CAPTAIN ROBINS
TO THE
RESCUE

The whole team was thrilled that
Charlie was going to help them. There
were six weeks before the starship
reached the next planet, so Captain
Robins let them use the big hold
for training.

Some of the other kids on the ship
were interested in soccer, and they came
to train, too. None of the new players
were as good as the original All-Stars.

Charlie was a good coach. He managed to sharpen their skills, and gave them confidence in their tackling.

"If only there was another team our own age we could play," Todd said to Charlie. "We could challenge the crew to a rematch, but I'm sure they would knock us flat again."

"I'm not so sure about that," said Charlie. "Finding another team your age is a problem. There can't be one closer than twenty light-years away."

The rest of the team agreed. Then, once again, Captain Robins came to the rescue.

CHAPTER 8

NEW
PLAYERS

A message arrived for Todd at school one day.

```
Report to the bridge.
16:00 hours today.

          J. Robins, Captain
```

Everyone in the school thought this was great. Almost no one got invited to the bridge by the captain.

The bridge was an amazing place, full of equipment to drive *The Searcher* through twisting wormholes in space. This was the only way the ship could travel between the stars.

When Todd arrived, a man's face was on a screen on the captain's desk.

"This is Mr. Wilson" said the captain. "He's on Astria. That's the planet we're heading for. I believe you play soccer on Astria, Mr. Wilson?"

"That's right," said Mr. Wilson, "but we're not very experienced yet."

"Neither are we!" said the captain. "Here's Todd, captain of our under-15 team. Can you give him a game?"

"We'd be glad to!" said Mr. Wilson.

A week later, *The Searcher* was in orbit over Astria. Astria was an ocean planet, with thousands of small islands where the people lived.

Soon the team was heading down in a shuttle craft. The crew's team was landing as well.

"Coming to support us?" asked Becky.

"No chance! We've got a game of our own. We've been challenged, too!" replied one of the crew members.

CHAPTER 9

WINNERS AND LOSERS!

The whistle blew. Todd passed to Mick. The Astria team expected him to pass back to Todd and a player moved to intercept, but the All-Stars were ready with a trick Charlie had showed them. Mick tapped the ball sideways to Tim, who kicked it up to Todd. Todd was ready for it.

Bang! Todd shot, but hit the cross-bar of the net.

That was close! The Astria players were surprised. The All-Stars were good!

Astria had the ball now, and Becky had to make one of her great saves.

She was ready for it, and the ball was soon moving the other way. Tony trapped it well, and passed it to Mick. Mick was in position. With a snap it was in the back of the net. Goal!

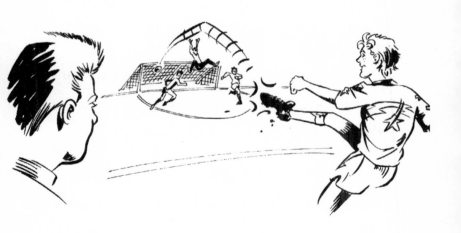

The All-Stars were up by two at half time. At the beginning of the second half, Astria made another goal. They were playing much better now.

Then Tim made a mistake in defense and let a ball through. An Astria player pounced on it and fired at the goal.

Becky didn't see it until the ball was in the back of the net.

The game was tied. Two minutes to go. Todd had the ball.

An Astria player came flying in for the tackle, but Todd used another of Charlie's tricks to dodge him.

All the Astria players were falling back now. Their keeper couldn't see the ball.

Todd shot the ball over their heads. The keeper jumped and missed. Three to two! The All-Stars had won!

Later, on the shuttle ride home, Todd's team saw that the crew team wasn't celebrating.

"Come on," said Becky. "Tell us how you did."

"We lost, seven to nothing," said Charlie. "That's not the worst part. They had cameras set up. Everyone on the planet was watching!"

★ ABOUT THE AUTHOR

David Orme taught school for 18 years before becoming a full-time writer. He has written over 200 books about tornadoes, orangutans, soccer, space travel, and other topics. In his free time, David enjoys taking his granddaughter, Sarah, on adventures, climbing nearby mountains, and visiting London graveyards. He lives in Hampshire, England, with his wife, Helen, who is also a writer.

★ ABOUT THE ILLUSTRATOR

Paul Savage works in a design studio. He says illustrating books is "the best job." He's always been interested in illustrating books, and he loves reading. Paul also enjoys playing sports and running.

He lives in England with his wife and daughter, Amelia.

★ GLOSSARY

bridge (BRIJj)—an area on a ship from which the captain controls the ship

crew (KROO)—all the persons who operate a ship

galaxy (GAL-uhk-see)—one of the very large groups of stars that are found in the universe

hold (HOHLD)—a part of a ship where cargo is stored

intercepted (in-tur-SEPT-id)—stopped

light-year (LITE-yeer)—distance that light travels through space in a year; 5.88 trillion miles

mission (MISH-uhn)—a special job

orbit (OR-bit)—the path a spacecraft takes around a planet or star

referee (ref-uh-REE)—an official in certain sports who enforces the rules

wormhole (WURM-hohl)—a tunnel or pathway. Some scientists believe that special wormholes in space can be used as shortcuts between distant planets and stars.

★ DISCUSSION QUESTIONS

1. Is this a story about living on a starship or playing soccer? What is the point of this story? Explain your answers.

2. How did you feel about the crew challenging Todd and his friends to a soccer match? Why?

3. The starship was huge! Talk about the clues that are given to show this and then discuss how you picture the starship. What does it look like?

★ WRITING PROMPTS

1. What words helped you picture the soccer matches played in this story? Write about a sport that you like to play and be sure to use words that relate to that sport.

2. Imagine living on a starship with your family. Describe what you'd do and what you'd miss doing. What would your life be like?

★ ALSO BY DAVID ORME

Something Evil

Dark Lake was dark and deep; the locals knew it was trouble. When the new city was built on its shores, people started disappearing.

Space Wreck

Stranded on an unexplored asteroid, things do not look good for Sam and Simon. With their ship out of action, the stranded Ghost Ship offers their only hope of escape.

★ OTHER BOOKS IN THIS SET

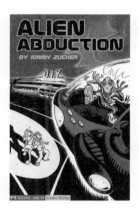

Alien Abduction
by Jonny Zucker

When Shelly and Dan are abducted by Zot the alien, they teach him about the ways of earthling teenagers. Hopefully they can convince Mr. Tann of their story before they end up in big trouble!

Big Brother at School
by J. Powell

The newly installed security cameras in the classrooms and the special "health check" day have made Lee suspicious. He is determined to stop his principal's mysterious plan before it is too late!